5 MINUTE DIGGER TALES

igloobooks

igloobooks

Designed by Tim Robins
Edited by Gemma Rose
© J.C. Bamford Excavators Limited 2018

An imprint of Igloo Books Group,
a Bonnier Publishing company
www.bonnierpublishing.com

Published in 2018
by Igloo Books Ltd, Cottage Farm
Sywell, NN6 0BJ
Manufactured in China. STA002 0418
10 9 8 7 6 5 4 3 2 1
Library of Congress Cataloging-in-Publication
Data is available upon request.
ISBN 978-1-4998-8208-7
IglooBooks.com
www.bonnierpublishing.com

CONTENTS

This JCB book belongs to:

JOEY'S BIRTHDAY BASH

It was a very special day at JCB HQ.
"Wakey-wakey, Joey!" called Roxy Robot. "Happy birthday!"
Joey JCB opened his eyes. "Thanks," he said, sleepily.

The rest of the team were busy organizing
a surprise party for Joey. Doug Dumptruck hung
party flags along the wall, Dan Dozer laid out food,
and Elvis Excavator set up DJ decks for a disco later on.

5

"Good work, team," said Doug. "Joey will love it."
"All we need now are the presents," said Tommy Truck.
"Where are they?" asked Max.

6

Doug looked around the room. He couldn't see the pile of presents anywhere. "They've gone!" he cried.

"Oh, no," said Marty Mixer. "Without presents, Joey's birthday will be ruined."

Doug told everyone to look for the missing presents.
The builders looked underneath boxes and scaffolding poles.

They searched the store shed and the
construction site, but found nothing.

Suddenly, Elvis spotted something in Marty's mixer.
"It's the presents!" cried Elvis, giggling.
"I don't know how they got in there," said Marty.
"Never mind that," said Doug. "We need to get ready!"

At last, everything was ready. "Joey's coming,"
said Doug, turning off the lights. "Everybody hide!"
Joey came into the room and the lights flicked on.
"Surprise!" shouted everyone.

"Thank you so much," said Joey.
"Here, open your presents," said Marty.
"You guys are the best," beamed Joey, as he
opened each gift. "This is the most awesome
birthday, ever, thank you!" Honk! Honk!

11

AMUSEMENT PARK FIASCO

The JCB Team couldn't wait to finish work. After a day of shoveling, lifting, and digging, Doug was treating them to a trip to the amusement park. They were so excited.

"It's going to be so much fun!" said Elvis.
"I'm going to whoosh down the Mega Slide!"
"Come on, let's go get our tickets," said Joey, excitedly.

As soon as they got through the gates, Dan Dozer and Elvis headed for the Mega Slide. At the top, they waved at the other builders. Dan went first. "Wheeeeeeeeee!" he cried, sliding down.

"Me next," said Elvis. It was going to be amazing!
He pushed off excitedly. "Wheeeeeeee!" Then suddenly,
Elvis came to a stop. "Oh, no! I'm stuck!" he called.

"Has anyone got a plan to get Elvis unstuck?"
asked Roxy Robot, worriedly. Everyone tried to think...
"I know!" volunteered Larry Loadall. "Leave it to me."

Larry climbed to the top of the slide, then slid down behind Elvis. He pushed his forks under Elvis's treads and lifted.

Larry released Elvis from the slide by lifting his forklift up high with Elvis sitting on it. Everyone cheered as they slid down to the bottom together.

"Thanks," said Elvis. "I thought I might be up there all night!"
"Good work, Larry," said Doug, as they headed to another ride.
"That's okay, no job is too big," said Larry with a smile.
"Now, let's have some fun!"

The builders spent the rest of the evening on all the cool rides.
They went on the merry-go-round, the haunted garage, and
the big roller coaster. "This is the most fun, ever!" said Elvis.

QUARRY RUSH

Joey and the JCB Team were working at Boulder Quarry and Joey was eager to get started. "Not so fast, Joey!" shouted Doug. "Gather around, I have an important safety talk before we begin."

Joey joined the others and listened to Doug. "The quarry
can be a dangerous place to work," said Doug, sternly.
"So, today we are going to pair-up with a work buddy.
And remember... safety first."

Joey was teamed with Marty Mixer.
"Come on, Marty," said Joey, eagerly.
"Let's move some rubble!" Joey whizzed
across the quarry into the old tunnels.
"Wait up, Joey!" replied Marty. "We have
to stick together!"

Inside the dark quarry tunnels, Joey started working hard.

He dug up rubble, moved rocks, and zoomed through
the tunnels, leaving Marty far behind. "Not so fast, Joey!"
shouted Marty. "Remember what Doug said!"

Joey was too far ahead of Marty to hear his warnings. "Too much rubble, too little—" But before Joey could finish, the ground beneath his wheels crumbled...

... *CRACK!* and he fell into a deep, dark hole!

"Help! Marty!" screamed Joey. But there was no reply. Joey was stuck in an old mine shaft. It was cold and wet, and Joey started to feel very scared.

Meanwhile, Marty had gone for help. The JCB work buddies searched the tunnels and before long, they found some skidmarks and... a large, dark hole.

"Help!" shouted Joey. "I'm stuck!"
"Don't worry, Joey!" said Doug. "We'll have you out in no time."

"I'm sorry, everyone," said Joey. "I was going too fast and I didn't stay close to my work buddy." "It's okay, Joey," replied Marty. "Now, let's be safe and move some rubble, together!"

SEASIDE ROCKS

The JCB Team were enjoying a day off at the sunny seaside! Joey had never been to the seaside before and he was super excited. "Come on, team!" shouted Joey. "Let's have some fun!"

Joey looked around the beach. There was so much to do!
"What should I do first?" thought Joey. He couldn't
decide, everything looked so much fun.

Joey joined Larry and Doug in the sea. But the waves splashed his wheels and water sprayed in his eyes.

He didn't like it, so he went to see Roxy at the rock pool. Then, a crab crawled out and made Joey jump with surprise!

Joey was determined to have fun. He parked next to
Dan on the sandy beach, but because he was wet,
sand got in his engine and gears.

"The seaside isn't as fun
as I thought it would be,"
moaned Joey.

Joey decided to go home. As he drove away from
the beach he noticed a big sign. "Wow! Now that
looks like fun!" thought Joey, and he changed
his mind and whizzed back to the beach.

Joey was finally having fun at the seaside. The sign had been for a sandcastle-building competition, and with a little help from his construction buddies, Joey was having lots of seaside fun building the biggest, best sandcastle, ever!

SNOWY MOUNTAIN

It was a cold and frosty morning high up on Snowy Mountain. The JCB Team were noisily hard at work, making a new highway through the snowy mountain peaks.

"Sssh!" said Joey, as the team stopped to listen. "We need to be quiet and careful. The snow is getting thick and we don't want to cause an avalanche!"

Dan started pushing, plowing, and piling up snow. He was clearing the way for his building buddies to scoop and move.

Dan was enjoying his job so much he got carried away and started to sing and yodel... "YODEL-AAY-EE-OOO!"

"Dan!" said Doug, sternly. "Didn't you hear what Joey said?"
"Sorry, Doug," replied Dan. "I was getting carried away. I love
clearing the snow and it's so beautiful up here."

But as soon as Dan was back plowing the snow,
he was back yodeling. "YODEL-AAY-EE-OOO!"
CRACK! RUMBLE! "Oh, no!" shouted Elvis. "AVALANCHE!"

The snow whooshed down the side of Snowy Mountain
and completely covered Dan, Elvis, and Doug.
"We're stuck!" cried Doug. "Look what you've done, Dan!"

Joey and Roxy heard the *CRACK!* and *RUMBLE!* and zoomed to the avalanche site. The snow had covered the whole area. "DAN! ELVIS! DOUG!" shouted Joey. "Where are you?"

Elvis and Doug could hear Joey, but Joey couldn't hear them. "I know," said Dan. "I've got an idea!" Dan cleared his throat and... "YODEL-AAY-EE-OOO!"

Dan's yodel was so loud that Joey and Roxy easily found their friends in the deep, cold snow.

"Sorry," said Dan. "I should have listened and worked quietly."
"That's okay," said Joey. "Now, let's get back to work. There's
a little bit more snow to clear!" The whole team laughed as
they cleared the snow and finished the new highway... quietly!

SPEED BUILDERS

The JCB Team were helping to build the new Speedway Racetrack. "This is going to be the biggest, quickest, and slickest racetrack, ever," shouted Joey as he started work.

Joey whizzed around, showing off his super speed. "If we had a race," he said to his co-workers, "I think I would win, because I'm the fastest builder in town!"

Elvis laughed. "Don't be silly, Joey," said Elvis, as he lifted a heavy load of rubble. "I am the most powerful builder, so I would win the race!"

Nearby, Marty Mixer
was busy mixing cement.
"Don't be silly, Elvis," he said.
"I'm super sleek and would
zoom to the finish first!"

Then, Dan weaved through
some cones. "Don't be silly,
Marty," he said. "I'm small
and whizzy! I would
win the race!"

Before long, the JCB Team had finished the Speedway Racetrack. "Shall we give it a test run?" suggested Joey. Marty, Dan, Joey, and Elvis all lined up ready to race.

"ON YOUR MARKS... GET SET..."
"Wait for me!" shouted Max, as he sped to the start line.
"Can I join in?" The team looked at each other and smiled.
"Of course!" they all cheered.

"... GO!" They were off! Joey... then Marty... then Dan... then Elvis, were all startled and left in a spin, as Max flashed past in a blur, and whizzed to the finish line first!

"Good race, everyone!" said Joey. "Well done, Max!"
"We might not be the fastest racers in town, but we are
the FASTEST BUILDERS!" The team cheered and looked
proudly at the brand new racetrack they had just built!